It was Saturday morning and Maya jumped out of bed. She was very excited because today was her birthday!

She skipped down the stairs. The smell of pancakes filled the air. She was in for a treat!

Maya filled her plate with some pancakes and strawberries. "What outfit will you wear to your birthday party today?" asked her mommy.

After breakfast, Maya searched through her wardrobe. She was not sure what to wear on this special day.

Maybe her jeans and a striped shirt?

Maybe her polka dot dress?

But then, a shiny outfit caught her eye...her purple lehenga.

Maya loved her lehenga! She loved the jewels on the blouse, and the sparkles on the long skirt. She put on the lehenga and twirled in circles. She felt magical!

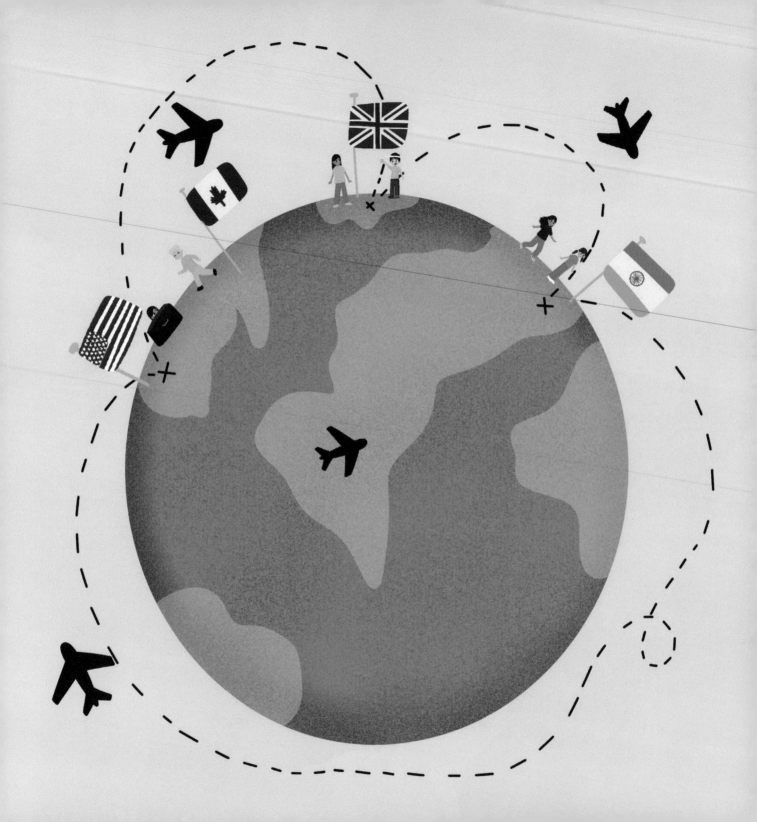

She remembered meeting her family from around the world at her cousin's wedding last summer. Everyone was wearing bright colors and shiny outfits.

She remembered helping her daddy to serve fluffy, yellow samosas and juicy, orange jalebis to the wedding guests. How tasty the food was.

She remembered spilling some dhaal on her lehenga. Oh dear! Luckily her grandmother cleaned her lehenga so that it looked new again.

She remembered dancing late at night, the stars were shining. She danced until her feet were sore!

She remembered not wanting the night to end. Even though she was sleepy, she felt happy.

How special it was to be with all of her family.

Maya was so happy to have these memories in her lehenga.

She smiled to herself in the mirror. She knew exactly what to wear to her birthday party.

"Happy Birthday!" cried her friends and family.

Maya blew out the candles and made a wish. She wished for new memories made in her magical, purple lehenga!

Printed in Great Britain
by Amazon